SIKA AND THE RAVEN

A Dr. H Book ™

BASED ON NATIVE AMERICAN LEGEND

written by Dr. Carl A. Hammerschlag

illustrated by Baje Whitethorne, Sr.

A TIPI Book For Kids

A Dr. H Book ™

The Dr. H book imprint is a trademark of Turtle Island Press, Inc. (TIPI)

Published by Turtle Island Press, Inc.
3104 E. Camelback Road, Suite 614, Phoenix, Arizona 85016

http://www.turtleislandpress.com

book illustrated by Baje Whitethorne, Sr.
book design by Beverly E. Soasey

First edition: April 1999

Hardcover edition ISBN: 1-889166-23-5

Publisher's Cataloging-in-Publication
(Provided by Quality Books, Inc.)

Hammerschlag, Carl A.
    Sika and the raven/written by Carl A. Hammerschlag;
illustrated by Baje Whitethorne, Sr.--1st ed.
    p. cm.--(Dr. H. books)
    SUMMARY: In this Native American legend, a young girl asks
Grandfather Turtle for a baby of her own, and is told she must
pass the test of keeping raven caged for a year.
    Preassigned LCCN: 98-61536
    ISBN: 1-889166-23-5

    1. Raven (Legendary character)--Juvenile literature.
2. Indians of North America--Folklore. 3. Responsibility in
children--Folklore. I. Whitethorne, Baje. II. Title.

    E98 F6H36 1999   398.24'528864
                                      QBI98-1390

            10 9 8 7 6 5 4 3 2 1

Printed by: C & C Offset Printing Co., Ltd.
            Hong Kong

Pronunciation Guide

Sian Kaan.........................SEE ON Kahn

Sika.................................SEE Kah

Eligio..............................el EE he oh

Abuela............................Ah BWAY lah

Luís................................Loo EES

qumbolimbo...................COME Bo LIM bo

For Hayley...my Tushy Princess.
CAH

———————◆———————

To my son Blaine, my granddaughter Tailor, and my mother Alice.
BW, Sr.

———————◆———————

TIPI is dedicated to publishing and marketing creative products
which enhance personal and community well-being.
We intend to inspire, teach principles of quality character and
contribute to charitable causes that preserve our natural resources.

TIPI

On the night I was born, my mother saw a shooting star so she named me *Sian Kaan*, which means "born of the sky." Everyone calls me *Sika* though. That's how my baby brother said my name, and it stuck. I live in a small village that is surrounded by cornfields. We cleared the fields out of the thick, dark jungle which surrounds us.

I love to go with Uncle *Eligio* to visit the people in our village. I call him Uncle Eli. He is a healer among our people. He keeps people from getting sick and helps people get well when they are ill or hurt.

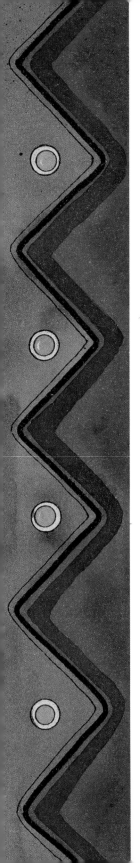

Today we go to see an old woman in our village. We call her *Abuela*. She tells Uncle, "If only my bones didn't ache so much, I could live forever." Uncle Eli winks at me as I help him wrap heated stones in palm leaves which he then places all over her body.

She sighs and tells Uncle Eli, "Ah! Now I can live forever."

Next we stop to see Anna and her new baby. Last night, the women of my village helped Anna deliver her new son, *Luís*, into the world. Today Uncle Eli will greet the newest member of our village and ask the Great Spirit to protect and guide him.

The newborn is so small and helpless. When I am allowed to hold him, he grabs my thumb tightly. Looking like a doll, he is warm and snuggles close to me. I love holding him.

After our visits in the village, we often go into the jungle to gather herbs, bark, and feathers. It's my favorite part of the day. Looking for these special things always makes me feel as if I'm on a treasure hunt. Every time I find something, Uncle Eli shows me how it is valuable because it has a purpose for healing.

"These leaves, Sika, can be burned to clean and heal us. The bark of the *qumbolimbo* tree can heal skin sores." He brings a tiny frog over. It is bright red with golden yellow sides.

"It is so beautiful, Uncle Eli."

"Yes, but its skin is poisonous and very dangerous. Do not eat animals of this color. And remember, Niece, that all things of the earth are sacred, every creature and every plant. The earth that supports us is sacred, and so are the stones. The stones are our most ancient relatives and speak to us through the steam in our sweat lodges. All this is given to us by the Creator."

We bring all the sacred objects back with us.
Uncle Eli sorts them and then
prepares them for medicines.

Sometimes, on the days we are together, I get tired and take a nap.
If I remember my dream, I tell Uncle Eli. He understands dreams.
He finds meaning in them which allows him to help people.

One day when I woke up from my nap, I remembered this dream.

I was holding my favorite doll. I laid her down next to me and as
I unwrapped the shawl around her, she turned into a real baby!
She smiled at me, and I picked her up. She was so warm and
delicate. I loved holding her.

I told Uncle Eli I would love to have my own baby.

He sighed, "Sika, my niece, you are not alone in that wish.
Let me tell you a story."

" . . .There was a time, long ago, when all the creatures and plants, the breeze, and the rain could speak to one another...the wind to the trees, the grass to the deer, and the Earth Mother to all her creatures.

A young girl lived among the creatures. She slept on beds of flowers, sang with birds, ran with the wind, and danced with the rain. She played with Deer and Squirrel, and Snake told her stories. She was happy in her family of all the jungle creatures, but she saw that she was the only creature with two legs. When she saw other newborn animals with their mothers, she started wishing for one of her own babies.

She went to see Grandfather Turtle, the oldest and wisest of all the animals, and asked him to help her get a baby of her own.

Grandfather Turtle said, "You are still very young yourself. It's not time for babies yet. It is a path that requires much patience. Small children are demanding. They are always asking for something. Besides, you are not alone. Look at everything around you. They are all your relatives."

"Please, Grandfather Turtle," she pleaded. "I have patience and could love and care for a baby."

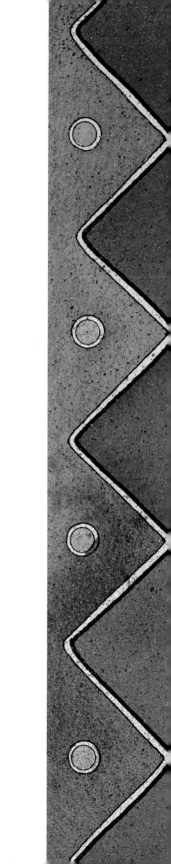

Grandfather Turtle was moved by her words. "I will give you a chance," he replied.

He told the girl that she must take care of a bird – a very special bird – which he pointed out to her in the corner of his hut. There inside a cage made of willow branches was a beautiful young bird. His feathers were so bright and iridescent, they glistened.

"This is Raven. He is young, but already he can sing more sweetly than Lark and speak more cleverly than Coyote. But no matter how he begs and sings, you must never let him out of his cage. If you can do this for one year, you may have a child."

The girl was so happy. She knew she could pass the test even if Grandfather Turtle thought it was too hard for her.

"I promise!" she replied. "I know I can do it."

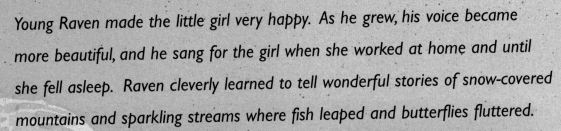

Young Raven made the little girl very happy. As he grew, his voice became more beautiful, and he sang for the girl when she worked at home and until she fell asleep. Raven cleverly learned to tell wonderful stories of snow-covered mountains and sparkling streams where fish leaped and butterflies fluttered.

Month after month, Raven pleaded with the girl, "Please let me out of my cage. Just once, that's all I ask."

The girl had come to love Raven. It hurt her to see how unhappy he was in his cage day and night. But she always remembered Grandfather Turtle's test, and no matter how much Raven pleaded, she never let him out of his cage. As he got older, his pleading became more insistent, and one day she just couldn't stand it anymore. She said to Raven, "If you promise me that you'll fly around the room just once and then come back, I'll let you out."

Raven promised, "Oh yes. I give you my word. Once around and then I'll return." The girl opened the cage.

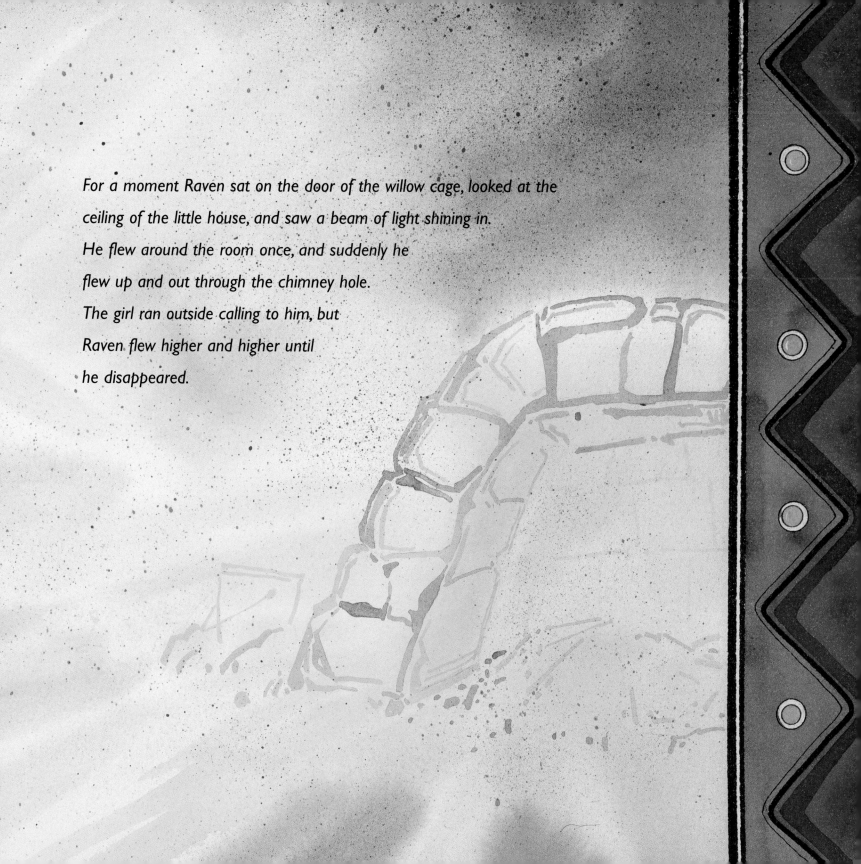

For a moment Raven sat on the door of the willow cage, looked at the

ceiling of the little house, and saw a beam of light shining in.

He flew around the room once, and suddenly he

flew up and out through the chimney hole.

The girl ran outside calling to him, but

Raven flew higher and higher until

he disappeared.

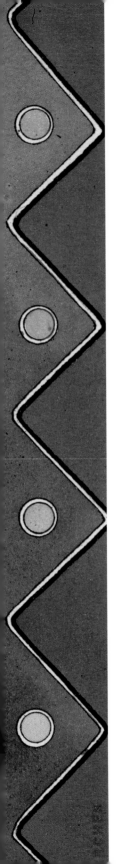

Her head bent in sorrow, the girl went to Grandfather Turtle and told him what had happened. She told him about her disobedience after Raven had made a promise to her.

Grandfather Turtle said, "You have learned much from your experience with Raven. You are not yet ready to have a child, but there will come a time when you will have a child of your own. For now, all Earth Mother's creatures are your family. Reach out and touch them, and let them find a home in your heart."

Then Grandfather Turtle summoned Raven. "Because you did not keep your promise, from this time forward, you will no longer sing or speak beautifully. You will repeat only a single cry, CAW CAW CAW, and your colorful feathers will be like chimney soot."

After Uncle Eli finished telling the story, he paused and looked at me.

"So that's why Raven is black and can't sing," I said.

"And why little girls don't have babies," Uncle Eli added.

"I guess I'll have to wait for a baby."

I liked Uncle Eli's story, but if Grandfather Turtle had given Raven
to me, I don't think I would have let him out.